Brooklyn
Doesn't Rhyme

Brooklyn Doesn't Rhyme

·∘꘏ JOAN W. BLOS ꘏∘·

Illustrated by
PAUL BIRLING

CHARLES SCRIBNER'S SONS • NEW YORK
Maxwell Macmillan Canada • Toronto
Maxwell Macmillan International
New York • Oxford • Singapore • Sydney

Charles Scribner's Sons Books for Young Readers
Macmillan Publishing Company
866 Third Avenue, New York, NY 10022
Maxwell Macmillan Canada, Inc.
1200 Eglinton Avenue East, Suite 200 · Don Mills, Ontario M3C 3N1
Macmillan Publishing Company is part of the
Maxwell Communication Group of Companies.

First edition   10 9 8 7 6 5 4 3 2 1
Printed in the United States of America

Library of Congress Cataloging-in-Publication Data
Blos, Joan W. 3-6 P Sharp
Brooklyn doesn't rhyme / by Joan Blos :
illustrated by Paul Birling.—1st ed.   p.   cm.
Summary: At the request of her sixth grade teacher, Edwina Rose
Sachs records events in the lives of her Polish immigrant family and
their friends living in Brooklyn in the early 1900s.
ISBN 0-684-19694-8
[1. Polish Americans—Fiction. 2. Jews—United States—Fiction.
3. Family life—Brooklyn (New York, N.Y.)—Fiction.
4. Brooklyn (New York, N.Y.)—Fiction.] I. Birling, Paul, ill. II. Title.
PZ7.B6237Bp   1994   [Fic]—dc20   93-31589

ACKNOWLEDGMENTS

Sincere thanks to Connie Regan-Blake and Barbara Freeman, storytellers par excellence; to Aliza Shevrin, Yiddishist and translator; and especially to Lilian R. Uviller-Pilat, whose interest and remarkable memory made these stories possible and this book more true.

To the memory of
Fanny Stark and William Biber,
immigrants

Contents

Miss Edgecomb 3

Grandparents, Uncles, and Aunts 8

Candy Babies 14

Dreaming Chicago 19

Pyro 27

Itzy 32

Johnny 39

Nothing at All 47

Justice 54

At the Library 61

Momma and the Vote 69

Itzy with a Difference 77

Important Dates, Names, and Events 86

*O*n the night before the first day of school, hair was washed, clothes were pressed, pencils were sharpened and ink bottles filled. Edwina Rose Sachs, nearly always called Rosey, carefully wrote her name and address in the printed spaces on the black-and-white cover of her composition book.

The school she attended was just a few blocks away, and the streets of its old Brooklyn neighborhood—Throop and Stuyvesant and DeKalb—bore the names of Dutch families who had lived there long ago. Now the people who lived there were mostly Jewish immigrants, newly come to America, hopeful and hardworking. It was their children who went to American schools and became Americans.

In past years Rosey's brother had the teachers first. "Oh, Edwina," they would say, using her formal name, "you'll have to work very hard indeed to do as well as your brother. Such a fine boy and so smart!"

But this year's teacher, Miss Rosalia Edgecomb, was new to the school and to teaching. And Rosey would have her first.

Miss Edgecomb

$\mathcal{M}$iss Edgecomb is beautiful and young, not like most of our teachers. She has smooth blond hair and a nose so pretty and thin that some of the girls, when they go to bed at night, put clothespins on their noses. This, they hope, will help them to grow up looking like Miss Edgecomb.

We like her because she is so pretty and nice, but Miss Edgecomb is often serious when she talks to us. After we pledge allegiance to the flag, she will usually ask us about the words we say.

"What is the meaning of *allegiance*?" she will ask. "Use the word *indivisible* in an original sentence."

Often Miss Edgecomb talks to us about democracy: how every man may vote in the elections and even those whose families are poor may be president some day. Miss Edgecomb forgets that, though being poor doesn't matter, being born in this country does.

Most of the pupils in my 6A class were not born in this country. So even someone smart like Itzy, who is my brother Arnold's best friend even though he is in my class, can never be president. Never mind, Miss Edgecomb says, it is all the more important that we be good citizens.

Another thing she talks about a lot is having respect for yourself.

"Class," she will say in her lovely voice, "if you wish others to have respect for you, you must first respect yourselves. Writing will help you to learn that. Pencils and notebooks, please!"

So that is why, in Miss Edgecomb's class, we do not write about "My Favorite Book" or how Abraham Lincoln, when he was a boy, walked five miles to school. We write about ourselves.

This is not as easy as it sounds.

The first time we had this writing to do, I could not think of anything to tell about myself. I was born in 1895 and my hair is brown. As these two things are also true for just about everyone in the class, they are not very interesting. The only one with blond hair is Julia Blankensmith. Since second grade we have been best friends, and her father is a doctor. I didn't think I could write a whole composition about that either. Then I tried to make a poem, but Brooklyn doesn't rhyme.

I was not the only one to have had such trouble in knowing what to write. So Miss Edgecomb reminded us to write about our families, too. And not just brothers and sisters. We should think about parents, uncles, aunts. Even our grandparents!

"Why," said Miss Edgecomb, smiling down at us, "even before the War of Independence one of my grandfathers was a scout for General Anthony Wayne. And after General George Washington became this country's president, my grandfather visited him. And my grandfather Bradford had many exciting adventures with his good friend Daniel Boone. We still have the knife that Grandfather Bradford used the night he discovered that, by mistake, he was sharing a cave with a bear!"

But who among us would have such stories to tell? Itzy was the one to raise his hand and, when called on, stand nicely beside his desk and explain to Miss Edgecomb that most of our grandparents are not in this country but still on the other side. And even if they were already here, you can be sure, said Itzy, they would not go calling on presidents or have such an adventure.

"But those are *my* stories," Miss Edgecomb said. "Your stories will be different. And knowing about your family will help you to know yourself."

We did not see how such a thing was true. But if our teacher said so, especially Miss Edgecomb whom we loved from the start, we would try to do what she asked. So that was when I started thinking about my life, I mean really *thinking*.

At first it was hard to know where to start or what to think about. Then I began to remember things that I probably hadn't thought of since the time they happened. I changed my mind about some of them. For example I began to like my brother more. And I realized that Momma, though she sometimes made fun of his ways, really liked our father. So, in that way, the remembering was a help, and not just with the stories.

I also learned that Miss Edgecomb was right. Because I am part of my family, knowing my family's stories is part of knowing myself.

Grandparents, Uncles, and Aunts

None of my grandparents came to America when my parents did. Later, they said, later. Year after year my grandparents wrote to my parents: When there is enough money, then we are going to come.

Everyone saved up money for the tickets—worked extra hours, bought nothing they did not need. Meanwhile my mother's father started a new business that he did not want to leave. The new business became a good business, and who would be so foolish as to leave that behind? It was one thing after another. One grandmother didn't hear so well anymore. The other grandfather died. After a while we understood. There would be no coming over.

When she thinks of this my mother's face is sad. It is hard for our mother that she does not think that, in her life, she will ever see her mother and father again. She has, it is true, a photograph in which they are smiling. But what is just one photograph from a photographer's studio half a world away? Except for letters that come to us once in a while, in languages I and my brother cannot read, we do not know how they are getting on, or if they are sick or well.

Although I know she is proud of us, it is also hard for our mother that often she cannot understand what we are learning in school. Momma does not read English and cannot read the books that we bring home. As for writing in English, she can only make her name.

Sometimes I think that Momma is not happy that she came to America, even though, if I ask her, she will say it is not so. Maybe because of missing her family she is always especially glad, and makes something good to eat, when Uncle Benny visits.

Our Uncle Benny is my mother's favorite brother. He came to this country after our mother and father did, and at first he lived with them. Uncle Benny came because it was hard for a Jew in Warsaw, where he lived, and also because of the stories about America. In America, it was said, everyone was rich.

Uncle Benny's wife is named Tante Ruth and this is how they met. In the spring that I turned eight, Uncle Benny came to us and told how he was walking in the rain on Forsyth Street in Manhattan. On this street there is a park on one side. On the other side are a cigar store, a candy store, and also several factories where small things are made. At the corner of Stanton Street they are building a school.

In one of the windows facing onto the street there was a sewing machine with a young lady sitting in front of it. She was making gloves. Uncle Benny saw her from across the street. Right away he stopped his walking and stood there and fell in love. He knew this was so because he forgot about the rain. Only when the rainwater dripped down from the brim of his hat and came inside the collar of his coat did he remember the rain.

So the next day and the next day, too, Uncle Benny couldn't help himself and went back to Forsyth Street. By this time the sun was shining. On the fourth day Uncle Benny waited until time for the shop to close. When the young lady came out of the shop he introduced himself. On the fifth day they went walking.

She also came from Warsaw. So, from the start, they had a lot to talk about. Also, Uncle Benny is very political—too much so, my father says—and so is Tante Ruth. Both believe in unions for working people—teachers the same as factory girls, women the same as men. Momma says that before she met Uncle Benny, Tante Ruth's life was hard. Sometimes you can feel the hardness in Tante Ruth's way of talking. I do not mind this in Tante Ruth because of what Momma said.

When Uncle Benny met Tante Ruth he did not have a job. For this reason, he did not have the money to show her a very good time. Every day, though, he would call for her. Sometimes they went to political meetings together. Sometimes they had a meal in a restaurant. At last they decided it was time to get married.

Right away Uncle Benny got a job making suits for men. He became a cutter, which he still is, and learned to take good care of his scissors, which could cut through three, maybe four, thicknesses of cloth at one time. Scissors are everything to a cutter. Uncle Benny was a fast worker and a good one. Since he was getting more and more pay he did not look for another place to work but stayed on working with the same manufacturer, whose name is Solly Cohen.

Uncle Benny's wedding was very happy and nice. The dancing was good and Tante Ruth laughed and cried, just as it is supposed to be for good luck in the marriage. Uncle Benny danced with her and me and my mother, and then my father joined in and we all danced around together. Sadie fell asleep and Tante Ruth's sister was holding her and smiling. Arnold was having a good time, too, and we stayed up very late.

Tante Ruth already had two boys when Uncle Benny met her, and now there is Rena-Rifka. This is what they call her: Rena-Rifka. It is a combination of her Jewish and American names.

When Uncle Benny and Tante Ruth got married people said that the husband she had before had gone off to look for work somewhere—maybe to Boston, maybe to Philadelphia—and then never come back. Momma says that Tante Ruth is not the only person to whom such a thing has happened.

Tante Ruth was lucky, I think, because Uncle Benny is so nice, and when Uncle Benny married her he took the boys as sons. They are older than Arnold, my brother, and sometimes we call them Yonkeleh and Herschel and sometimes Jack and Harry, as they are called in school.

Uncle Mendel is my other favorite uncle. We call him that even though he isn't really an uncle but only the brother of my father's sister's husband. He can be very funny.

Once, when he came to visit us, he hired two hansom cabs. Uncle Mendel rode in the first of the cabs and, in the second one, what should there be but Uncle Mendel's hat!

Uncle Mendel is a worry to our father because often he has to borrow money, sometimes from our father. So why, he asked him, had he done such a thing as hire two hansom cabs?

"Oh," said Uncle Mendel, "so that you will remember."

"Remember what?" asked my father. "That besides being extravagant, which we already know you are, you are also foolish?"

"No," said Uncle Mendel, "that even a poor man such as I can for fifteen minutes live like a Rockefeller."

You would not think that two such different people as my father and Uncle Mendel could be in one family—ours. But, of course, it is also true that they come from different sides of the family and are not very much related.

Candy Babies

*O*n the day my baby sister was born I wanted to buy her a present. I didn't know what to get her because I didn't know much about babies. Finally I decided to buy some candy babies. At the corner store I spent one cent: half of my week's allowance. It did not buy as many chocolate babies as I had hoped it would.

When I explained what they were for, Mrs. Wessel, who owns the store, laughed behind the counter and Mr. Wessel, who owns it, too, added a few more candies to those already in the bag. So then it was nice and full. Then he folded over the top and twisted out the corners, closing it up tight.

I carried those chocolate babies very carefully, so as not to melt them. I did not put my hand around the bag. When I got home the house was very quiet. No one was in the kitchen, and my mother's door was closed. I thought she must be sleeping and the baby was in her room. I imagined that the nurse who was staying to help take care of the baby was sitting beside the bed. The nurse and the doctor had come to the house to help the baby get born, and now the nurse would stay with us until my mother felt better. Maybe the baby was in her lap. Maybe my mother was holding the baby close to her in bed.

I was lonely for my mother and for my brother, who was not at home, and for my father, who had not gone to work that day until after the baby was born. I went and sat in the parlor so I could watch the street.

It had started to rain, a little, and the street was shiny and wet. One or two cabs and a carriage went by, and a few delivery wagons. I wondered if I would see any automobiles and thought about how, if we were in the street, we would run after them and yell, "Hey, mister, get a horse!"

I still had the bag of candies.

After a while I opened the little paper bag and looked in at the babies. It was dark and cozy in there with a kind of brownish light that came in through the paper. I began to think to myself, She is such a little baby. She will never notice if just one of them is gone. So I ate one baby.

I folded over the top of the bag, just as Mr. Wessel had done, and twisted the corners out. It looked just as it had. That baby I ate very slowly. The chocolate tasted thick and warm and, for a long, long time, I could feel it in my mouth.

After a while I began to look out the window again. It wasn't yet time for the lamplighter to come, just starting to get dark. I told myself I would not eat any more candies but I could not help thinking about them. Then I saw the lamplighter and then I ate one more.

Now two babies were gone. I told myself that because of the extras Mr. Wessel had given, I still had left one whole penny's worth of babies and that was a good present.

I wished my mother would wake up and ask me what I had learned in school that day and if I had behaved. I wished my brother would come home and start to practice the piano. While I was wishing this, I ate two more babies.

After I ate these babies I did not fold over the top of the paper bag the way I had done before. So now it was easier to reach inside and take another baby. And I did.

That was when I stopped counting how many of them I ate. I just sat there, with no lights on, eating chocolate babies. After a while I couldn't taste the chocolate and I wasn't hungry. Even so, I kept on eating those babies, one right after the other until not one was left.

I looked at the empty bag and I was sure that if anyone found it they would know what I had done. Even if I bought them with my own allowance money, I should not have eaten those babies.

I put on my hat and coat and walked out on the street. It had stopped raining. I walked for three blocks under the lit lamps. Then I crumpled up my little paper bag and put it into someone else's garbage can. Then I walked home slowly.

All the lights were on. The baby nurse and my brother were both in the kitchen. It looked like they had been laughing.

Arnold asked, "Where'd you go, Noodle?" (This was an old nickname of mine.)

The nurse said, "It was very wrong of you—going out without telling anyone. Your mother needs her rest now and should not have to worry about where you are."

But I did not tell them where I had gone or what I had done—not even when the baby nurse looked at me in a kinder way and said, "Now that you have a brand-new baby sister you must set a good example because she will learn from you."

I went upstairs to my room and began to think about what I could teach my baby sister when she was old enough. I thought about my jump rope and my pencil box. Then I got out the book of poems that my father had given me, with a poem he wrote himself, when it was my birthday. The book had print that was very little and pages that were thin. When you pressed the covers of the book together the gold on the edge of the pages looked like solid gold.

Most of the poems I did not understand, though I loved the sounds of the words. Then I remembered the one about a cloud, and a laughing child, and a piper. That poem would be good, I thought, for a little sister to have. I began to feel happier when I found that poem. I put a marker in the book and then I went downstairs.

Dreaming Chicago

If I come home with my stockings torn again or my brother loses his pencil box again and needs it to be replaced, Papa will look at Momma and say, "They are sending me to the poorhouse. The poorhouse is where I will die."

We aren't supposed to believe this, and we don't. We aren't rich like Julia Blankensmith's family but neither are we poor.

Julia Blankensmith is my best friend. When we met in second grade, we both were scared of the teacher. Julia's mother is tall and very thin and almost as blond as Miss Edgecomb, who is our teacher now. Julia's mother wears beautiful clothes and writes poems for magazines. Sometimes she goes to meetings about changing the laws in this country so that women can vote. Julia's father is a doctor and his office is in their house. So it isn't like Julia's family with us, but neither are we poor.

It is only because she wants to that Momma makes our clothes. And we always have help with the house. Every Monday Mrs. Doherty does the wash and, on Tuesdays, she irons. To help with the cooking and cleaning there is always a girl. These girls who help us are older than I am but it makes no difference. We always call them girls. Mostly they come from Poland, which was Momma's country before she came to America and got married to my father, who came from Austria.

Usually, before a new girl comes, we get a letter telling us be sure to treat the new girl nice and what a wonderful person—so hardworking—she is going to be. This letter will be written by a relative of hers or a friend of her family. How do they know us, to write us such a letter? We always find out later that this relative or friend also has a relative or friend acquainted with some person in our family. That is how it goes. And the letters almost always end with some information about our relatives. Sometimes we are not supposed to know the things that are told us in this way, but that is all right, too.

The girls, when they come, stay in the third-floor bedroom, just above the second-floor room that I share with my baby sister. Listening to their footsteps I can tell when they get up from the chair or walk across the room. Sometimes they cry with homesickness at night, and I hear that too. In the morning, their eyes still red, they come down and talk to Momma, saying how lonely they are. That day Momma is quiet with them, gives them the best part of the meat, makes little jokes—in Polish. Only Momma can talk to them at first but even the loneliest of our girls never go back to Warsaw or Krakow or whatever their town had been. After they know some English they move away from us. They find a job in a factory and rent a room somewhere. Soon there is a boyfriend. Most of these girls are not with us very long, and it is for this reason I hardly remember their names.

With Bogdana it was different.

The first time I saw Bogdana I was sitting on the stoop. I did not know how she would look, but Momma had told me to go and wait so that is what I was doing. We had the usual letter, this one from a relative who said that the ticket had already been bought and that we should expect her on such and such a date. It also said that Bogdana had a son, a little boy just four years old, and he was coming, too.

Sometimes we would go to meet the girls when their boats were landing. But this time Papa, in answer to the letter, sent Bogdana our address. She should come when she arrived. How, we asked, could she even

ask how to get here, not knowing English yet? Papa said not to worry. If she could travel to America from Poland, she could travel from Manhattan to Brooklyn, which is where we live.

The first thing I thought, when I saw her down the block, was that she walked like a queen. No other girl, coming to work for us, had given me this impression. It didn't matter that this queen had a child, a pale boy who looked frightened, or that her shoes were heavy, or that a fringed shawl covered her head and lay across her shoulders on top of her dark wool coat. I, of course, had never seen a queen—only the pictures in my books—and that didn't matter either. Bogdana looked like a queen to me. A fine queen. In disguise.

In one hand Bogdana carried a large bundle. It was thickly wrapped in a blanket or a rug and tied around with rope; the other hand carried a suitcase, also large, that was covered with leather. The little boy also had something heavy to carry: a covered wicker basket nearly as big as himself. At the same time, with his one free hand, he was holding tightly onto his mother's skirt.

I could see her looking at the numbers on the houses and then at the paper she held in the hand that also held the bundle. A smile began when she got to 305. It grew as she passed 307 and then the one next door to us, which of course is 309. At 311 she put the suitcase down, and the little boy did the same with his too big basket.

"Good morning, my name Bogdana!" she called, right away using up four words of the English she knew. Then she reached into a pocket and held up a page with writing. I could see our address on it, clearly printed out. It was the letter Papa had sent to her! How far that letter has traveled, I thought. And here it is back to us.

"Please?" she said, saying it as a question and using up one more word.

"Come in," I said. "You are here."

Bogdana moved in quickly and well, which was how she did everything. Her room became a little home, even having its own, and special, smell, and she made a pile of blankets in the hall as a bed for the little boy. Arnold said he should have an American name and began to call him Charlie.

Speaking in Yiddish, Papa made the joke that maybe his real name had been left behind and was still in the old country! Maybe it would be there if he ever went back! Charlie looked at his mother when we laughed, still so little he thought it might be true. No, she was telling him, no. But if he was to be a real American boy he must have an American name.

Likewise, Charlie's father, Janek, was spoken of

as Johnny. With Bogdana, though, you took her as she was. Bogdana's name stayed Bogdana, was never made Bessie or Blanche. At first I had not liked the name and found it hard to say. Later it seemed beautiful to me, like Bogdana herself.

Charlie's father had come ahead of them and was working in Chicago. There he'd saved up the money for their crossing. When he had saved up again, and could buy their tickets for the train, they would join him. Bogdana and Charlie had a game they liked to play about going to Chicago. Charlie would begin it.

"What do in Chicago?"

Bogdana would say: Have car.

Charlie: With horn?

Bogdana: With horn.

Charlie: With lights?

Bogdana: With lights.

Charlie: Four wheels?

Bogdana: Four wheels, and shiny leather seats!

"And I will sit with you and my papa in front?" Charlie would always ask this question though the answer never changed.

"No, my little one, you will sit in the back. And your papa the driving will do."

This would start Charlie frowning but not for very long.

"Then," he would say, looking up at his mother, "if you will sit with Papa in the front, I will blow the horn!"

The game about cars was Charlie's favorite. Bogdana liked better the one about the house that they were going to have.

"And will our water come again from the well, as it did at home?"

"No, my little one, no. In America we all have water that comes by itself to the sink."

On they would go, naming the fine advantages of an American house. Gaslight. Indoor plumbing. Maybe, one day, not too long, even a telephone. (We had only recently gotten ours, and the voices that spoke to us out of the black machine were a wonder to Bogdana and, indeed, to us all.)

But car or house or the fine clothes they would wear, the place was always Chicago. I might wish that Bogdana would stay in Brooklyn. But, as Bogdana explained it once, "Johnny and I, ever since we are married, are all the time dreaming Chicago. Everywhere people have dreams," Bogdana said, "but only in America do such dreams come true."

And that was when I understood that Bogdana and her Johnny, like my parents and my Uncle Benny, had not come to America because of a car or a house. They had come to find a dream. One day I would, too.

Pyro

"But how did you and Papa get together?" I ask Momma one day. We are in the kitchen and Momma is making noodles to go in the chicken soup.

The kitchen has a homey, floury smell. Momma's sleeves are rolled up high and little pieces of noodle dough are sticking onto her hands. Momma's arms are fine and strong—not thick and hairy like our Tante Anny's but not bony either, like Julia Blankensmith's mother's.

When Momma does not answer my question, I ask it again.

"How did you and Papa—?"

"Too alone," says Momma, which is all the answer I get.

I should have known not to ask. Papa, not Momma, is the one to tell us stories. English is trouble for Momma, we do not like it when she talks Yiddish to us; Polish we don't understand. But not in any language is Momma a teller of stories. It is not the way she is made.

"But now you are not alone," I say, suddenly loving my mother. "You are not lonely now?"

"No, my little one," Momma says to me, with her beautiful smile. And even though she has flour on her hands and will not have touched me, I feel as if she had hugged me, which, in a way, she has.

One day Momma and I and Bogdana were together in the kitchen. Charlie and Sadie were having their afternoon naps, and Arnold was not at home.

"Go," said Momma when the doorbell rang; and when I went to answer, there was Uncle Benny. He had a strange look on his face and there was something bulging in the pocket of his coat.

"Is Momma here?" he asked me. He didn't even give me a hello. Just: Is Momma here?

So we went back to the kitchen where Momma and Bogdana were getting dinner ready.

"*Nu,* Benny," said Momma when she saw him, meaning "Benny, what now?"

So Uncle Benny took his left hand out of his coat pocket and there was a spotted dog. Right then it wasn't much of a dog, just a handful that did what puppies do when they are little and frightened.

So Bogdana got a floor rag and quickly cleaned

up the mess, and Momma and Uncle Benny sat down, and I sat down, too. The puppy was on the floor beside us, going around on the wooden floor, his toenails making little clicks and his tail straight up in the air.

"At the fire station across my street," Uncle Benny explained, "the dog surprised the firemen with having too many puppies. This one, that one, they were giving away. So my Yonkeleh, which he shouldn't have, said he would take one, too.

"Yonkeleh is a good boy, very kindhearted," my Uncle Benny continued.

"Just like you," said Momma. "But Ruth doesn't want the puppy. Tell me if I'm wrong."

"So I thought that you, with such a nice back-yard—" Uncle Benny looked helplessly at Momma, who did not answer him.

"His name is Pyro," Uncle Benny said. "Means *fire* in Greek, I think."

"Greek I don't care for," said Momma, "and a puppy I don't need. Benny, Benny, when will you *think* before you are saying yes?"

"But think how I am lucky!" said Uncle Benny. "With such a wife and two fine lovely boys—"

"—and a puppy," said Momma firmly.

Meanwhile Bogdana had given the puppy some milk and I got down to practice calling his name, and Uncle Benny left.

For some days all went well. Papa was fond of Pyro, it turned out, though he wanted to call him Duke. So Momma said that the puppy could stay so long as she was not the one who had to take care of him. Where Momma grew up, dogs were animals; the same as sheep and cows and pigs. They did not belong in the house.

Arnold, my brother, and Itzy, his best friend, made plans to build a doghouse so Pyro could sleep outside. It was going to have a pointed roof and a window, with glass, at the back.

Then Pyro snapped at Sadie, or maybe Charlie, and Momma said, "No more Pyro," and would not change her mind. Each of us had a different idea for Pyro, but with Momma it was no use.

Then, on a Saturday afternoon, Uncle Mendel came. It was the Sabbath when we are forbidden to ride so he had walked to us this time, no carriages or cabs.

As soon as Uncle Mendel walked into the house, Pyro ran to him. It was as if, for Pyro, an old friend had come back. He wagged his tail and made half jumps in the air and little puppy nips.

"See how he likes you," said Papa to Uncle Mendel, unnecessarily.

"So, Mendel," said Momma, not wasting any time, "a dog would be good for you, living alone; good company, no trouble."

And before Uncle Mendel could make much of a reply, Arnold was sent for Pyro's collar and leash, and Momma had packed up for Pyro his bowl and a nice big bone.

I think Uncle Mendel liked the idea and Pyro certainly did. Still, we were sad when Uncle Mendel left, taking with him the puppy that we'd had such a little time.

"So what do you think," asked Papa, "Mendel now will come to us with *three* hansom cabs?"

For a moment we were puzzled. Then we saw what he meant.

"One for him, one for his hat, and one for Pyro!" we shouted.

And Momma, when we looked at her, was smiling at our father with love in her beautiful eyes.

Itzy

*I*tzy Carnitzsky is the unfortunate name of my brother Arnold's best friend. Usually it is hard to know just when a friendship begins. With Julia, it was after we moved, so I was in second grade. But who can say exactly when and why we started to walk together after school let out? Or when we first bought penny candy together and shared what we had bought? Or I went to her house or she came to mine? But Arnold, my brother, knows exactly how it was that he and Itzy Carnitzsky started to be friends.

One day in October, the same year Momma gave Pyro to Uncle Mendel, my brother went to the iceman to get a new piece of ice. For the kind of icebox that we have, we need ice twice a week. Instead of paying to have the ice delivered, my brother Arnold goes to the iceman's place and brings the ice home in his wagon. From all the ice it has carried, the inside of his wagon is not so bright and shiny as it used to be. Folded in the bottom of the wagon is a woolen blanket. The blanket is old, with moth holes, so we do not use it for bedding anymore. The blanket, which is blue, is to put on top of the ice until Arnold gets it home. Once our little sister asked how it can be that a blanket, which keeps us warm, keeps Arnold's ice pieces cold?

On this particular afternoon our mother gave Arnold five cents for the ice, which is what she always did, and told him not to lose it, which she also always did. It is about a twenty-five-minute walk to the place where we get our ice.

When Arnold got to the iceman's place the iceman said there were no more five-cent pieces. Too much trouble, the iceman said, for such a little money. So now there were only ten-cent pieces, which, to be fair, were bigger.

This would not have been so bad. But in his pocket my brother had only the nickel that Momma had given to him. It would take him nearly forty-five minutes to go back home and return. It was not a nice day to be out, cold and windy and dark.

"Aw, mister, please! Just this time?"

It did not take much to make the man lose patience.

"Sonny," he said, "you want ice, I got ice. But for ten cents, like I told you. You don't got ten cents handy, you don't get no ice. Go, I got customers waiting."

It was true. Several boys bigger than my brother were there, with dimes to pay for their ice. From the way they were looking at him my brother hoped, for a minute, that one of them would be kind enough to lend him the needed nickel. But he couldn't think of how to ask and no one made the offer.

So, with his wagon, my brother was standing there, thinking what he should do. If he came home and brought no ice, Momma would be angry. If he stayed late and maybe could borrow a nickel or maybe buy a little piece of ice if there was one left over, Momma would be worried. Either way he thought of it, my brother was not happy.

My brother now noticed another boy who seemed about his age. This boy was wearing foreign-looking clothes and pulling a much-used wagon.

"What's your name?" the new boy asked. "Mine's Itzy," he went on.

What this Itzy wanted to explain was that, like Arnold, he had just five cents. And he needed ice.

Surprising my brother with the good English he spoke, Itzy quickly continued, "To me he said the same as you. So supposing you give me your five cents, I buy for both of us a ten-cent piece, and then, when he has given it, I say very quickly, 'Please mister, knock it in half.' "

"I don't know," said Arnold. "Supposing he remembers you? And besides, I never saw you in my life. How do I know you won't just take my nickel and run off with the ten-cent piece?"

"Me?" asked the boy. "With a name like Itzy Carnitzsky, would I do such a thing?"

The way he said it was sad and funny both. So Arnold gave him the nickel, and Itzy bought the ice, and the iceman, when he realized what had happened, started to be angry but didn't yell very much.

From that time on Arnold and Itzy bought their ice together almost every week. For a while, in the coldest middle of the winter, Itzy made some kind of an excuse about needing no more ice. From this we all of us understood: The Carnitzskys were short of money. Food would keep cold on the windowsill. And whatever money they saved in this way would help to buy the coal for the stove with which they heated their flat.

When Arnold first met Itzy, he lived in the neighborhood next to ours and went to a different school. Then Itzy's family had to move and that is when Itzy had to change schools and started to be in my class. Arnold is still best friends with him and when Itzy is visiting at our house I am friends a little. Mostly I do not have friends who are boys or know what to say to them.

There came a time when Miss Edgecomb asked me if something was wrong with Itzy and would I please inquire. Why, Miss Edgecomb, wanted to know, was he coming to school one week and then missing the next? One week in, one week out.

I didn't know how to ask Itzy myself. So finally I told Arnold what Miss Edgecomb had said to me and asked him to ask Itzy.

The answer made me sad. Itzy's father had once more lost his job. And Itzy and his brother were having to share between them one good pair of shoes. For Itzy the shoes were a little too large; for the brother, already in high school, maybe a little too small. One week Itzy, one week his brother. One week in, one week out.

"Itzy says not to worry," Arnold said. But no one else that we knew of had to share their shoes. And with such news about a friend who would not be worried?

For the first and only time I told a fib to Miss Edgecomb. I told her I hadn't been able to find out why Itzy wasn't in school.

For some time Papa had been telling us that people were starting to worry that they would lose their jobs. There were too many greenhorns coming over, they said; even in America there could not be work for everyone when there were so many who were coming at one time. We had heard our parents arguing with their friends. Some would say, "No more immigrants!"

But then others would ask them, "So who are we to talk?"

Always Papa's answer was the same: "Maybe now we are having some hard times. But America, don't you forget it, is still a thousand times better than what we had before." Then Papa would look around and say, "Here a good man still finds work."

But Itzy's father, who was surely a good man, was not finding work.

In the end it was Papa who helped. One of Papa's customers was a big manufacturer who made ladies' clothes. He needed a man to take the finished garments from the factory where they were made to the stores where they were sold. He told Papa he was looking for a man as honest as he was strong; the last man he had was a liar and the one before that was so weak he was always complaining at what he had to carry.

Papa promised this gentleman that Abe Carnitzsky was more honest than a rabbi and as strong as two Samsons together. No one blamed him for this exaggeration and, about the honesty, it was absolutely true.

We were proud of our father for helping out, and with Mr. Carnitzsky again at work, another pair of shoes could be bought and Itzy came back to school. As to who would get the shoes, it was reasoned that Itzy's feet would grow, so Itzy wore the shoes they already had, and his brother got the new pair.

Johnny

When Bogdana first came to live with us with her little boy Charlie, there would be a letter from Chicago almost every week. That is where her husband was working, saving up the money he earned so they could come there, too. After a while his letters came not so often. Then nothing for a month.

We could see that Bogdana was afraid that what had happened to our Tante Ruth was happening to her. Maybe her Johnny was no longer hoping for her and Charlie to come. Maybe he had found some nice American girl; maybe a greenhorn wife like Bogdana would be an embarrassment. Then there came one more letter. After that, no more.

Now, from Bogdana, there were no more laughing stories, and from the little third-floor room we did not hear them playing "What do in Chicago." In the house was a sadness, and all of it came from Bogdana. Sometimes she would forget for a little while; more often she could not even eat—not even, as Momma said, worrying, enough for a little bird.

When at last I had my good idea I had to be surprised with myself for not thinking of it before. It was getting to be springtime. I told myself that I would wait until after we had our seder. If, after Passover, Bogdana wasn't better, then I would do my idea. In the meantime I could only hope that one day we would find Bogdana back to her happy self.

I am so unlucky with my wishes that, before a picnic, I wish for it to rain. Then, maybe to spite me, the sun will shine that day. So I tried wishing the opposite: Don't make Bogdana better. Even though I did it, I did not expect that it would work and, of course, it didn't.

Sadie was really the youngest. But it was decided that Bogdana's Charlie, who was next to the youngest, was going to ask the Four Questions at our Passover that year.

Papa helped him practice the words and to say them in the right way. Meanwhile Bogdana and Momma made all the preparations. Arnold and I kept mostly out of the way. And then it was Passover.

All of the family that lives in Brooklyn came, and also some from New Jersey whom we do not know as well. Altogether it made twenty-two people and so twenty-two places were set, ten of them at a separate table which was for the children.

When all of us were seated, Papa began the service. When he came to the part where Charlie asked the questions, Charlie was called from his place at the children's table to stand up next to Papa.

"Wherefore," he began in his high little voice, not yet perfect in English, "is this night different from all other nights?"

We could see that Papa was smiling at Charlie to encourage him. "Any other night," we heard Charlie say, speaking the words we knew and loved so well, "we may eat either leavened or unleavened bread, but on *this* night only unleavened; all other nights we may eat any kinds of herbs, but on *this* night, only bitter. . . ."

When Charlie came to the end of his part you could feel how happy we were that Charlie did not forget what he had learned or make even one mistake.

Bogdana was smiling, almost in her old way. So, for that one night we were happy. We said to one another how glad we were that she was in good spirits. But the next day she was sad once more and again not wanting to eat.

As I had told myself I would, on a day soon after the seder, when the weather was nice, I said to Momma that I had to return a book to the library. Then I said that Charlie should come with me. I was starting to teach him to read, and I wanted to show him the books.

Then I said that Bogdana should come too, in case I had to take too long finding a new book. This part was a fib. I meant to go to the library, but that wasn't all. I did not like to tell a fib, especially to Momma, so I crossed my fingers when I was saying this. Luckily Momma had decided to think that fresh air was good for Bogdana. She told Bogdana to go with me, and so Bogdana came.

When we got to Sumner Avenue, instead of turning to the right, which would have taken us to the library, we went the other way.

"Later, comes the library," I said, crossing my fingers again. "There is something we must do first. It's just a few streets more."

Charlie was always obedient and Bogdana seemed too tired even to argue with me. We walked the next blocks hardly talking at all. Then, talking very fast, I said, "Bogdana, this is my friend Julia's house. Please come with me, Bogdana, because we are going to see her father, who is Dr. Blankensmith."

Bogdana was looking angry.

"Bogdana, please, it's for Charlie," I said, which, in a way, was true.

We went in the door that Julia had plainly told me I must never, never use. It led to a room, where dark-colored chairs were arranged around the walls. A table was in the middle. The people who were waiting there all looked up together when they saw us coming in. Only a few looked sick.

I saw two chairs that were empty. I crossed the room to get to them, and with Charlie lifted onto Bogdana's lap the three of us sat down.

The nurse had a stiff white uniform and an even stiffer hat.

"Oh," she said when she saw us. "I do not think I know you. Have you an appointment with Dr. Blankensmith?"

"No," I said, "but we have to see him. Please, it's very important."

"It's always important, seeing the doctor," she said. "That's why you need an appointment. These other people, they all have appointments. If I let you see him without an appointment everyone without an appointment will want to see him, too."

Just then another door opened and Julia's father came out. A stethoscope was around his neck and instead of a regular jacket he was wearing a long white coat. He didn't look like Julia's father now. He looked like a doctor.

"Why, Edwina," he said to me, "what are you doing here?" He wasn't looking as angry as the nurse, just surprised and not very pleased.

So right in front of everyone I explained about Bogdana. The nurse kept interrupting to say that we had no appointment. All the other patients were starting to look at us, too.

"Nurse," said Dr. Blankensmith, "I think I will make an exception and see this young woman now. Please, if you will excuse us," he said to the other patients. And Bogdana and Dr. Blankensmith disappeared through the door.

I was so scared for Bogdana! I took Charlie on my lap and while we sat there I was counting in my mind how much we might have to pay. I had brought my saved-up holiday money and the fifteen cents that was my whole allowance for the last three weeks. I was ready to promise to save up all my allowance until I had enough.

After what seemed a long, long time Bogdana came out alone. I couldn't tell from looking at her if she was feeling better.

"Come," said Bogdana, taking Charlie from me, and walking straight to the door. I knew enough just to follow her out. But as soon as we were on the street I had to know what happened.

"So, Bogdana, is it medicine you need?"

"No, my Noodle, not medicine. 'One round-trip to Chicago,' he said, 'to be taken at once.' "

Right in the street I hugged her because Bogdana

had started laughing and crying both and I didn't know which was on top.

It was only when we were halfway home that I remembered the money. Bogdana said she had asked about that herself. "But my dear young woman," he had said, "how can I charge you money, when I gave no medicine?"

After that, everything happened. Momma didn't mind my fib and Papa lent Bogdana the money and Bogdana went to Chicago right away where Charlie's father was. Charlie stayed with us meanwhile and he and my sister, who was then three years old, kept Momma hurrying.

In Chicago, as we later learned, Johnny had lost the woodcarver's job he had. Even though it was not his fault, Johnny was ashamed. When he found another job it did not pay good money and was not in his line of work. That was when he had written the letter that Bogdana so badly misunderstood: "When I have something good to write, then I will write again."

Together in Chicago they had laughed at the mistake. But Johnny was saying all the time that he was sorry, so sorry to have made Bogdana sad.

Not long after Bogdana returned to us Johnny wrote a new letter. He heard that in the city of Detroit a Mr. Ford was hiring people for his new company. Johnny was going to Detroit and he promised to write from there. Next, from Detroit, there came a long, good letter, which Bogdana read aloud to us, translating into English as she went along.

It was like a story in a book, how everything turned out! Bogdana and Charlie soon went to Detroit, and before the end of another year Johnny was making good money.

They rented a house near other Polish people, and Bogdana wrote long letters to us about her American home. When they could afford it, they bought a second-hand sewing machine. Soon Bogdana, with piecework to do at home, was earning money, too. Because of this it wasn't even two years before Johnny bought a car. And sure enough, it had headlights and a horn, just as in Charlie's game.

Nothing at All

*I*t is said in our family that jokes, not people, are for laughing at. But once, just once, it was different.

Before we moved to our Hart Street house, which is where we are living now, we had just a flat. A nice flat, but a flat. It was across the street from the park, but the street was noisy with traffic. So when Papa was doing better in his business, he bought for us a house. It was not a big distance from the third-floor rooms we rented to our new three-story house. But the new block was a nicer one, with trees; and although the houses were all the same, 311 seemed special because we knew it was ours.

"Here," said Papa, showing it with pride, "there will always be room enough—no more Momma's sewing machine pushed into Arnold's piano. And for you, little Noodle, who already writes fine stories, a desk with pigeonholes!"

At that time I was in class 2A, and although I had trouble writing with ink I was fond of setting down stories and fonder still of Papa's admiration when I showed him what I had done. Arnold was in 3B then and our sister Sadie was not yet one year old.

Papa was careful to keep his promises, even the ones for which Momma scolded him as costing too much money. So Arnold looked forward to having more room for his piano and I to having a desk. It was easy to be happy about the move and we almost forgot to be sorry about the place we would have to leave.

For Momma, it was different. Where we were living she had good friends and she liked, and trusted, the neighbors. Maybe the flat was crowded, a little, but she had a place for everything and every window had curtains that she herself had made. For these, and other reasons besides, Momma had no wish to move.

As it happened we would have to move just before going to the mountains for the summer but after school was out. Never mind that we'd been in this school since each of us had started first grade, knew the names of the teachers, and looked forward to the fall when we would return. The new school, Papa promised, was going to be better.

"And who," asked Momma, "will speak to all these schools, make the arrangements to change?"

"You'll see, it will be nothing," said Papa. "And the children will gladly help."

It was the same with all that had to be done: Say good-bye to our landlord and explain why we were moving from where we had lived five years; make sure the moving men would come; pack, in borrowed boxes and barrels, our clothes and all our bedding, our dishes, pots, and pans.

"It will be nothing," said Papa. "You will see, it is nothing at all."

So Papa went to business every day and Momma attended to everything, and when it came time for the packing, I and Arnold helped.

At last came moving day!

Early in the morning the moving men came with their wagon. In the back were old green blankets in which to wrap our furniture and Momma's sewing machine. We could see that the horses' feed bags had been freshly filled with oats. The horses were eating quietly. Soon, on the pavement beneath their feet, there began to be yellow circles of oats that had spilled out on the street.

After an excitement when he could not find his hat, Papa said a nice good-bye and left at the usual time.

"You'll see," he said to Momma. "The move itself will be nothing, really nothing at all."

For most of the day the moving men were busy. First they must carry down from our flat everything we had made ready—the boxes and barrels we had packed; the chairs and beds and mattresses; the kitchen table where we ate our meals; the bundles of linens and clothes. Each time they filled the wagon the men would start up the horses and take that load to our new house. Then, with Momma holding the baby, we would travel by trolley in time to meet them there.

Then Momma, with her key, would unlock the big front door and the moving men would start to empty the wagon, slowly carrying into the house the boxes and barrels, the chairs and the beds, and all the rest of it. Three whole times this happened.

Momma had imagined it so much in her mind that she knew exactly where each thing should go. Maybe for her it was not a surprise. For me and Arnold it was like a magic show to see the new and empty house turn itself into our home.

It was the same with the food. Momma had a plan for it in her mind and so, at lunchtime, there were sandwiches; for supper she had taken along plenty of boiling potatoes to be eaten with sour cream.

As soon as the moving men had gone we went downstairs to the kitchen. Momma found the pot she needed to start the potatoes boiling. While we were setting the table, putting plates and glasses and silver-ware out, Momma said first to make a place for Papa, then in another minute to take it away again. From this we knew that Momma was worried for Papa but angry at him too.

"Go," she said, when we had set the table, "and look out on the street. Maybe Papa is coming."

If my brother and I were not also worried we might have noticed how nice it was—the brown stone stoop and painted iron railings, the carving over the windows of the parlor floor. As it was, we looked up and down the street, not knowing the direction from which Papa would come. We waited for some minutes.

When we went back in we knew it would just make trouble to tell Momma about the men we'd seen who were coming home from business, taking the keys from their pockets, opening their doors. So we only said, "No Papa."

And Momma said only, nodding, not smiling, "I guess we don't need Papa to show us how to eat."

So then the three of us sat down, no one saying anything for thinking of Papa so hard. Even the baby was quiet. It seemed a long time after that, but was really just a few minutes until we heard the front door being opened and Papa was calling down to us, "Good evening, I am here!"

Arnold and I are lucky because our house, and not just the kitchen, is usually a good place to look for rubber bands. This is because our father's business is selling jewelry to customers who cannot pay all at once. Our father collects the money a little at a time. He goes to the customers' houses, visits a little, maybe has something to eat. It is not like some of the jewelers who are always in fights with their customers. With my father it is always a friendly matter, and my father's customers always pay what they owe.

At night, at our kitchen table, our father arranges the money that he has collected. The coins he puts in separate piles: ten dimes, twenty nickels, four quarters—each pile making one dollar. (The pennies he sorts by tens.) Then he puts together the piles to make maybe five dollars' worth of nickels or ten dollars' worth of dimes. The bills go into bundles: one-dollar bills (a lot of these), five-dollar bills, once in a while some tens. And this is where the rubber bands come in. Because around each of the bundles of bills he puts a rubber band. We do not ask Papa to give us the rubber bands. That would not be right. Still, if he happens to drop one on the floor and we are the ones to find it, then it is finders keepers.

By and by, when the center is ready and you have some rubber bands saved up, you begin to make the ball. At first, when you are covering up the foil, the

"So," said Momma, as he settled at the table and she brought him his food. "So what happened that you are here so late?"

"So I have to tell you," Papa said, and he reached out for our mother and caught her by the hand, "when I finished at work today I took the trolley like always and, like always, went home. Everything there was very nice and quiet, maybe just a few children jumping rope in the park. I had the key to open the downstairs door and even went up the stairs, three flights, so much was I forgetting—"

"—since," said Momma, laughing despite herself, "the move for you was nothing, really nothing at all!"

Justice

Yonkeleh wasn't our cousin until his mother, who is now our Tante Ruth, married our Uncle Benny. Yonkeleh was older than Arnold and I, being already a student at Boys High, where he was known as Jacob and still more often called Jack.

As my brother Arnold was all too often reminded, Yonkeleh was not only an excellent student but a member of the Debate Society, which was very exclusive. Perhaps it was because of this that everything that Yonkeleh said, even a *please* or a *thank-you*, turned itself into a speech. It took only one sentence, sometimes less, for this to begin to happen. So already people were saying that Yonkeleh surely would go to Columbia College and make a big success. Meanwhile he practiced being a success on Herschel, his younger brother, and sometimes on Arnold and me.

The year Uncle Benny and Tante Ruth got married

Yonkeleh got the idea in his head to make a rubber-band ball. He plainly told Herschel that the ball was going to be for the two of them. So Herschel promised he would help, and so did my brother Arnold who liked Herschel a lot. If Arnold would help then so would I. So that made three of us helping; but Yonkeleh was the boss.

Making a really good rubber-band ball is not so easy to do. It starts out with some silver paper foil, which you have to collect. The foil, which is very, very thin, you scrape off the wrappings of certain kinds of candy, maybe packaged tobacco, and sometimes baking chocolate. You roll up the first piece tightly so it makes a little ball. Then you keep adding layers of foil until you have something about the size of a green pea or a marble, only not a shooter, which would be too big. You press the foil tightly together so it is even and firm. This is the center of the ball, and it gives the finished ball the weight and balance it needs.

While you are still finding the foil and making little center, you start to look for rubber bands to the rest of the ball. Maybe one will be lying o street. You quickly stoop to pick it up and pu your pocket. Maybe one you will find in scho the pocket it goes. Or when Momma carries ceries home, if something was wrapped with band you quickly ask for it.

rubber bands are way too big and you have to twist them over and over to make them stay in place. Gradually the ball gets bigger than a walnut, then the size of a peach. Then it grows more slowly. Each rubber band goes only once or twice around and does not add much thickness. When you can only use the largest rubber bands, which of course are the hardest ones to find, it grows most slowly of all.

But now it is time to think of something else. How is it to be covered when it gets to be the right size? Some boys use it just the way it is, which doesn't look very nice. Some get their mothers or their older sisters to crochet a plain white cover made of crocheting cotton so thick it looks like string.

But the mothers of boys who are really fortunate, the boys whom good luck favors, their mothers make initials. Yonkeleh wanted initials—his; and so, of course, did Herschel. The problem was that Yonkeleh wanted *Y* and Herschel wanted *H;* both wanted *S* for Silverberg, which is their last name. There seemed to be no way out of it until Yonkeleh, one sunny afternoon, persuaded his brother Herschel to agree to a new idea.

This we learned about later when a smiling Yonkeleh brought the finished ball around to show for our approval. At first we could not understand why Herschel had not come.

Then we looked at the brand-new ball itself. It had a *Y* for Yonkeleh, and also it had an *S*. The *Y* and the *S* stood out clearly—blue letters worked on white.

"But," we asked, confused by what we saw, "is it not also for Herschel?"

"Yes," said Yonkeleh, "there is the *S* for Silverberg, his name, and the *Y* for me."

We were speechless at this argument and felt sorry for Herschel who, we felt, had been tricked. As if he could read what was in our minds, Yonkeleh said quickly, "We shook hands on it."

Even so, we thought he should not have done it. But Yonkeleh was fair about sharing the ball with Herschel, and after a while we pretty much forgot the unpleasantness with the initials.

After school, at that time of year, the boys would play stickball until it was time for dinner, and after dinner too. There wasn't much traffic on the side streets near the park. And if, sometimes, a wagon or a carriage came through, the game would stop for a moment and continue after it passed. Once in a while there would be an automobile. This was always taken as an event and talked about later on.

On this particular night, it was starting to get dark. The street lamps had already been lit and, between them, the street was filled with shadows which made it hard to see.

Arnold had given up his turn to hit and another boy from down the street positioned himself with the broomstick they were using as a bat. Herschel pitched the ball to him and *whomp!* it left the broomstick going fast, curved as it traveled the length of the street, and came down into the window of the corner candy store. It was where I bought the chocolate babies the day my sister was born. We all heard the sound of the breaking glass—the boys who were playing, Julia and I who were watching, even some neighbors who came out of their houses to see what had made the crash. None of the boys who were playing took so much as a step.

So what should happen but there came Mr. Wessel carrying the ball. Because we are all his customers, living in the neighborhood, he knows us all by name.

"You," he said to Yonkeleh, "look what you have let to happen with this ball belonging to you. One of the other boys, I could understand." Mr. Wessel's expression plainly showed that he thought they were lacking in brains. "But you—Yonkeleh!—always so smart! Going to Boys High!"

By now we were sure the police would soon be coming. We imagined our Yonkeleh going before a judge, being sent away.

So it was a big relief that before our thoughts had gotten any worse, Mr. Wessel said he would not call the police. But Yonkeleh would have to find a job and pay for what it was going to cost to get the window fixed.

It took Yonkeleh most of the summer to earn the full amount. Working for his uncle, a butcher, he had to get up at five o'clock each morning to make early deliveries. But he never complained, never argued, never asked for help. I think that in his heart he believed that justice had been served.

As a debater the following year he made a very good showing, leading his team to victory on the subject: Resolved that Logic, Not Chaos, Rules the Universe.

As for Mr. Wessel, we never found out for sure whether he knew that the ball that broke his window really belonged to both Silverberg boys or just the older brother whose initials it displayed.

"So," said Momma, as he settled at the table and she brought him his food. "So what happened that you are here so late?"

"So I have to tell you," Papa said, and he reached out for our mother and caught her by the hand, "when I finished at work today I took the trolley like always and, like always, went home. Everything there was very nice and quiet, maybe just a few children jumping rope in the park. I had the key to open the downstairs door and even went up the stairs, three flights, so much was I forgetting—"

"—since," said Momma, laughing despite herself, "the move for you was nothing, really nothing at all!"

Justice

Yonkeleh wasn't our cousin until his mother, who is now our Tante Ruth, married our Uncle Benny. Yonkeleh was older than Arnold and I, being already a student at Boys High, where he was known as Jacob and still more often called Jack.

As my brother Arnold was all too often reminded, Yonkeleh was not only an excellent student but a member of the Debate Society, which was very exclusive. Perhaps it was because of this that everything that Yonkeleh said, even a *please* or a *thank-you*, turned itself into a speech. It took only one sentence, sometimes less, for this to begin to happen. So already people were saying that Yonkeleh surely would go to Columbia College and make a big success. Meanwhile he practiced being a success on Herschel, his younger brother, and sometimes on Arnold and me.

The year Uncle Benny and Tante Ruth got married

Yonkeleh got the idea in his head to make a rubber-band ball. He plainly told Herschel that the ball was going to be for the two of them. So Herschel promised he would help, and so did my brother Arnold who liked Herschel a lot. If Arnold would help then so would I. So that made three of us helping; but Yonkeleh was the boss.

Making a really good rubber-band ball is not so easy to do. It starts out with some silver paper foil, which you have to collect. The foil, which is very, very thin, you scrape off the wrappings of certain kinds of candy, maybe packaged tobacco, and sometimes baking chocolate. You roll up the first piece tightly so it makes a little ball. Then you keep adding layers of foil until you have something about the size of a green pea or a marble, only not a shooter, which would be too big. You press the foil tightly together so it is even and firm. This is the center of the ball, and it gives the finished ball the weight and balance it needs.

While you are still finding the foil and making this little center, you start to look for rubber bands to make the rest of the ball. Maybe one will be lying on the street. You quickly stoop to pick it up and put it in your pocket. Maybe one you will find in school. Into the pocket it goes. Or when Momma carries the groceries home, if something was wrapped with a rubber band you quickly ask for it.

Arnold and I are lucky because our house, and not just the kitchen, is usually a good place to look for rubber bands. This is because our father's business is selling jewelry to customers who cannot pay all at once. Our father collects the money a little at a time. He goes to the customers' houses, visits a little, maybe has something to eat. It is not like some of the jewelers who are always in fights with their customers. With my father it is always a friendly matter, and my father's customers always pay what they owe.

At night, at our kitchen table, our father arranges the money that he has collected. The coins he puts in separate piles: ten dimes, twenty nickels, four quarters—each pile making one dollar. (The pennies he sorts by tens.) Then he puts together the piles to make maybe five dollars' worth of nickels or ten dollars' worth of dimes. The bills go into bundles: one-dollar bills (a lot of these), five-dollar bills, once in a while some tens. And this is where the rubber bands come in. Because around each of the bundles of bills he puts a rubber band. We do not ask Papa to give us the rubber bands. That would not be right. Still, if he happens to drop one on the floor and we are the ones to find it, then it is finders keepers.

By and by, when the center is ready and you have some rubber bands saved up, you begin to make the ball. At first, when you are covering up the foil, the

rubber bands are way too big and you have to twist them over and over to make them stay in place. Gradually the ball gets bigger than a walnut, then the size of a peach. Then it grows more slowly. Each rubber band goes only once or twice around and does not add much thickness. When you can only use the largest rubber bands, which of course are the hardest ones to find, it grows most slowly of all.

But now it is time to think of something else. How is it to be covered when it gets to be the right size? Some boys use it just the way it is, which doesn't look very nice. Some get their mothers or their older sisters to crochet a plain white cover made of crocheting cotton so thick it looks like string.

But the mothers of boys who are really fortunate, the boys whom good luck favors, their mothers make initials. Yonkeleh wanted initials—his; and so, of course, did Herschel. The problem was that Yonkeleh wanted *Y* and Herschel wanted *H;* both wanted *S* for Silverberg, which is their last name. There seemed to be no way out of it until Yonkeleh, one sunny afternoon, persuaded his brother Herschel to agree to a new idea.

This we learned about later when a smiling Yonkeleh brought the finished ball around to show for our approval. At first we could not understand why Herschel had not come.

Then we looked at the brand-new ball itself. It had a *Y* for Yonkeleh, and also it had an *S*. The *Y* and the *S* stood out clearly—blue letters worked on white.

"But," we asked, confused by what we saw, "is it not also for Herschel?"

"Yes," said Yonkeleh, "there is the *S* for Silverberg, his name, and the *Y* for me."

We were speechless at this argument and felt sorry for Herschel who, we felt, had been tricked. As if he could read what was in our minds, Yonkeleh said quickly, "We shook hands on it."

Even so, we thought he should not have done it. But Yonkeleh was fair about sharing the ball with Herschel, and after a while we pretty much forgot the unpleasantness with the initials.

After school, at that time of year, the boys would play stickball until it was time for dinner, and after dinner too. There wasn't much traffic on the side streets near the park. And if, sometimes, a wagon or a carriage came through, the game would stop for a moment and continue after it passed. Once in a while there would be an automobile. This was always taken as an event and talked about later on.

On this particular night, it was starting to get dark. The street lamps had already been lit and, between them, the street was filled with shadows which made it hard to see.

Arnold had given up his turn to hit and another boy from down the street positioned himself with the broomstick they were using as a bat. Herschel pitched the ball to him and *whomp!* it left the broomstick going fast, curved as it traveled the length of the street, and came down into the window of the corner candy store. It was where I bought the chocolate babies the day my sister was born. We all heard the sound of the breaking glass—the boys who were playing, Julia and I who were watching, even some neighbors who came out of their houses to see what had made the crash. None of the boys who were playing took so much as a step.

So what should happen but there came Mr. Wessel carrying the ball. Because we are all his customers, living in the neighborhood, he knows us all by name.

"You," he said to Yonkeleh, "look what you have let to happen with this ball belonging to you. One of the other boys, I could understand." Mr. Wessel's expression plainly showed that he thought they were lacking in brains. "But you—Yonkeleh!—always so smart! Going to Boys High!"

By now we were sure the police would soon be coming. We imagined our Yonkeleh going before a judge, being sent away.

So it was a big relief that before our thoughts had gotten any worse, Mr. Wessel said he would not call the police. But Yonkeleh would have to find a job and pay for what it was going to cost to get the window fixed.

It took Yonkeleh most of the summer to earn the full amount. Working for his uncle, a butcher, he had to get up at five o'clock each morning to make early deliveries. But he never complained, never argued, never asked for help. I think that in his heart he believed that justice had been served.

As a debater the following year he made a very good showing, leading his team to victory on the subject: Resolved that Logic, Not Chaos, Rules the Universe.

As for Mr. Wessel, we never found out for sure whether he knew that the ball that broke his window really belonged to both Silverberg boys or just the older brother whose initials it displayed.

At the Library

It is hard to remember that when my sister was born I did not even like her. Now our Sadie is four years old and I love her with all my heart. I like to take her places with me and, when strangers smile at her, it makes me happy, too. With Arnold, my brother, it is different though he also likes her a lot.

One thing my brother and I did together was to teach our sister a poem. It was the one that we said each year in school to celebrate Washington's Birthday on February 22nd. Even though we learned it in first grade, we still say it now. When the whole school recites it together, and we stand with our hands held over our hearts, it sounds very patriotic.

Two years ago, when she was two, we taught the poem to Sadie to make a surprise for our father who likes patriotic things. When we told Momma what we had done, she smiled and said that an American family such as we were becoming should eat special that night.

She had heard that there was, on the other side of Brooklyn, a store where they sold strawberries even in February. She took the trolley there and back and, sure enough, for dessert that night we had strawberries! With cream. We did not tell her, Arnold and I, that George Washington, in the story, chopped down a cherry tree. For Momma it was all the same—strawberries, cherries, peaches. Good American fruits.

When it was time for Sadie to say the poem, we lifted her onto the table. The lamp hanging over the middle of the table shone its light on the top of her head, making Sadie's tight blond curls look as purely golden as everyone said they were.

"Go on, Sadie," we said to her. And standing there on the table, looking not at all afraid, she said it, every word:

> I love the name of Washington,
> I love my country, too.
> I love my flag, the dear old flag,
> The red, white, and blue.

The rest of us clapped our hands when she was done, Momma and Papa loudest, then Arnold and I. Such a good time we had!

It was not long afterward that I taught Sadie the poem I found on the day she was born. That was when

I thought I didn't like my sister and I ate up all the babies because I was lonely and sad. I think that teaching those poems to her helped me to like my sister.

Even when she was very, very little I used to take Sadie with me when I went to the library. She could be very quiet when I told her to.

The library is warm in winter and, in summer, cool. The Reading Room, which you come into first, has tall, high windows in front. From these windows you can see the park just across the street. Sometimes, when the weather is good, I go there after the library and start to read my books. When Sadie comes along with me I sometimes read aloud to her while we are sitting there.

In the library the first thing you probably notice is the old-book smell. Things that are old do not usually smell nice. But with old books it is different.

The Reading Room has bookshelves around the walls, and tables and chairs in the middle. Each table has six chairs. Mostly old men sit there, quietly reading their books. Maybe they like to come here and read; maybe they are ashamed for themselves not to have work to do.

The tables and chairs and bookshelves are made of yellowish wood. So are the door frames and windowsills, and the librarians' desk. The desk has a large calendar on one side and a lamp that works by electricity on the other side. Usually, in the afternoons, the sun comes in through the windows and the room looks golden because of the sunlight on the wood, and its yellowish color.

In the library it is quiet. Because of this you can hear small sounds—card catalog drawers sliding shut, people moving the chairs in which they are sitting, books being stamped with the date when they're due back, and the special librarians' stamp being put down on the desk. You can hear the swish of the librarians' skirts when they walk across the room finding books for people or doing library work.

The librarians have clean hands and soft voices. Most of the time they whisper. It might not sound nice to have them be so quiet but mostly it makes me feel peaceful, like just before falling asleep. I sometimes think about what librarians do when they are not being librarians. It is hard to imagine them buying food in stores, carrying home the packages, and starting to cook their dinners.

My favorite book is *Little Women,* which I have read three times since I was eight. I also like *Mrs. Wiggs of the Cabbage Patch, Rebecca of Sunnybrook Farm,* and parts of *Water Babies.* My brother Arnold likes *Hans Brinker and the Silver Skates* and *Toby Tyler.* My sister likes *Peter Rabbit.* Already she reads some words by herself and she likes to look at the pictures while I read my books.

To get your own library card you have to write your name, in ink, in a special book they have, and also on the card. Each name has to fit a little space, and if you make an ink blot they make you write it again.

When I decided to teach my sister how to write, it was mostly so she would be able to have her own library card. This was partly for her sake but also partly for mine. You are only allowed three books at a time and I did not like to use up one whole choice with taking out *Peter Rabbit.*

At first, when I started teaching her to write, she kept turning the *S*'s around and wanting to write just *Sadie,* instead of writing *Sarah Jane Sachs,* which is her real name. So then I explained about nicknames and Papa calling me Noodle when I was a baby. I could see that this was mixing her up so I told her never mind. Instead, I showed her the four *A*'s in her name: two in Sarah, one in Jane, and one more in Sachs.

After she could write her name, we practiced writing it small. All of this took many days to learn, and also the writing with ink.

Papa was proud of us both.

"See," he would say to Momma, "already our Noodle is starting to be a teacher. And the little one also is smart!"

At last I thought she was ready.

That day Momma combed Sadie's hair by curling it around her fingers into special long curls. I was excited for Sadie, but scared, too, underneath. I washed Sadie's hands just before we went so they were very clean.

When we got to the library I had to tell the librarian that we had come to get Sadie her first library card.

"Oh, little girl," the librarian said, "your little sister is much too young for that! Maybe next year you could try. She has to be able to write her name neatly, small, and in ink."

"I know," I said, "and she can."

I could see that she thought I was fibbing. But then Sadie, who was listening, said in a library whisper, "Please, I could just try."

"Well, all right," the librarian said. "But be careful with the ink. It will be most unfortunate if we have a spill."

Next we had to get a chair and stand it near the librarian's desk so Sadie would be high enough when she wrote her name. When I lifted her onto the chair, I realized how little and light she was and I started to be afraid that after all the work we'd done she would not get her card.

By this time another librarian had come to see what the first one was doing, and some of the men were looking up from their books to see what was happening. Sadie stood there quietly, writing her whole name. First she wrote it on the card and then in their thick, special book. I thought about how my name was in that book, only many pages back, and all the other names.

"Very good!" the librarian said when Sadie finished writing. "What kind of books do you like?"

"Oh," said Sadie, whispering, "when I was little I used to like *Peter Rabbit,* but now I like poetry."

This last answer surprised me but I tried hard not to show it.

"You do?" said the second librarian. "And what kind of poems do you like?"

"Well," said Sadie, thoughtfully, "the first one I learned was a surprise for my Papa but I can say it for you."

"That would be very nice, Sarah Jane," the librarian said.

And Sadie did, whispering, while I held my breath. By now the two librarians were smiling at my sister and asking her, in whispers, if she knew any more poems.

"Oh, yes," said Sadie. "It is by William Blake."

And then and there she recited the one that starts out with the valleys wild; the one about the piper who meets a little child.

When Sadie finished reciting, the librarians clapped their hands. Right there, in the library, they clapped their hands for my sister Sadie, and some of the men did, too. I think it was probably the only time that such a loud noise of clapping was heard in that quiet place.

Momma and the Vote

When Papa decided it was the modern thing to do we got a telephone. When it rang, which was not very often, Papa would answer it. He would hold the receiver tightly and press his mouth to the mouthpiece.

"Hello! Hello! Who's there?" he would shout, not quite trusting the telephone to carry his voice unassisted to whoever it was that was calling. Perhaps it was all this shouting that kept his conversations short.

If the telephone rang when Papa was not at home, my brother Arnold would answer. At such times Arnold enjoyed himself and he spoke without the shouting. But people were not calling us up in order to talk to Arnold. So Arnold's conversations were also very short.

Momma, from the start, had not wanted a telephone. Momma favored the ways she had always known. Take carpets. When Momma wanted the carpets cleaned, she and the girl who was with us at the time would take the carpets one by one and hang them over the line in back, the line on which, every wash day, Mrs. Doherty hung the clothes. There the carpets would be beaten by hand, using Momma's wire beater. Never mind that we also had a Bissell carpet sweeper. It wasn't the same, Momma said.

Or chickens. For a few cents more the fresh-killed hens we bought could be cleaned of their feathers by the butcher or his son. But Momma plucked our chickens herself, down to the little pin feathers that were hardest to get out. We never questioned Momma because there seemed nothing to question. Momma had always plucked the chicken feathers and so, we knew, had her mother.

So then, the telephone. It was, she said, an extravagance. What purpose did it serve, she asked? What could be so important that it must be said right away? Besides, she argued, it seemed to her not natural to be speaking with a person who was somewhere else.

Papa heard what Momma had to say but he bought the telephone. And Momma might have changed her mind just because Papa was so happy and proud: a very American thing to do, this owning a telephone. But Momma's first time using it she said "Hello" to the earpiece, and we could not keep from laughing. This gave Momma hurt feelings. She would not answer the telephone again until a long time afterward. And then she did not enjoy it.

In the house of Julia, my best friend, it is just the opposite. It is Julia's mother who likes the telephone most. When Julia's mother isn't writing her poems she goes to a lot of meetings. These are not the same as Uncle Benny's meetings about unions, or Tante Ruth's meetings at the Equality League of Self-Supporting Women about why women who work for wages should be paid the same as men. Mrs. Blankensmith went to college and she belongs to something called the New York Collegiate Equal Suffrage Vote. Her meetings are about women and voting. But maybe there is not so big a difference in the meetings after all: Some are about women being paid the same as men and some are about voting the same as men, and, as Mrs. Blankensmith says, it is all about being fair. Why she uses the telephone is to help arrange the meetings.

Julia's father is older than Papa, but her mother is younger than Momma. Julia's parents kiss each other right in front of Julia. They like to go to parties and they laugh a lot. The telephone is one of the things that they laugh about. This is because they got the telephone so Dr. Blankensmith's patients would be able to call him up sometimes instead of coming to see him when the weather is bad outside or they are very sick. But most of his patients don't have telephones in their houses, and the rest are so used to coming to the office they do it anyway. Julia's parents think it is very funny—why they got their telephone and who is using it.

One day the telephone was ringing in our house and, because Papa was not there, Arnold answered it. Right away you could tell from his voice that Arnold was surprised.

"Momma," he said, "it is Mrs. Blankensmith. She wants to talk to you."

Momma was in the kitchen chopping chicken livers, onions, and hard-boiled eggs in a wooden chopping bowl.

"You're sure?" asked Momma. "There is no mistake?"

"No mistake," Arnold said.

So Momma wiped her hands on a cloth and went into the hallway where we have the telephone. Arnold and I were listening hard but we could not tell, from what we heard Momma say, what the telephone call was about.

When she returned to the kitchen Momma said, "On Thursday Mrs. Blankensmith will take Julia to a lecture. Her organization and Tante Ruth's are making the meeting together. So she is hoping that I will give permission so she will take Noodle, too."

"Oh, Momma! And what did you say?" I asked.

"I said I would ask Papa." And Momma picked up the wooden bowl and chopper and started in again chopping up fine the livers and onions and eggs.

Papa surprised us by saying I could go. And the next day I told Julia. Not only was I being allowed to go with her to the lecture, I also had permission to stay overnight at her house. I do not know which made us more excited, but while we were deciding what we were going to wear we thought of nothing else.

To get to the lecture, which was in Manhattan, we had to take first the trolley and then the subway train. It took us an hour to get there. Most of the way going there Julia's mother sat between us and told us all about voting and that partly she was working so hard so Julia and I would be able to vote when we were grown-up women.

While we were waiting for the lecture to begin she told us about the lecture hall itself and the famous people, such as President Lincoln, who had spoken there. Sometimes Julia's mother sounds just like a teacher.

I did not see Tante Ruth at the lecture, which was really several lectures. Julia and I liked Rose Schneiderman's part the best, and who should we see, right away after that, but our teacher Miss Edgecomb! Sometimes I think that Momma and Papa and maybe our Uncle Mendel are the only people in the world not going to such meetings.

On the way home Mrs. Blankensmith asked what Momma thought about voting. I said that Momma did not often go to meetings but I thought she would like to vote. Momma, even more than Papa, worries about things like the earthquake in San Francisco and politics in Russia.

After dinner Julia's mother suggested that I might like to telephone to my parents. That way I could tell them that I was safely home. I did not want to admit to her that this would be my very first time to talk on the telephone. Luckily for me, the operator came on right away and I told her our number. I knew how to do this from watching other people.

Papa's voice came over the wires loudly, "Hello! Hello! Who's there?"

"Papa, Papa! It's me! It's me!" I was saying everything twice and shouting back at Papa. But after I stopped myself doing this, it was like regular talking.

"So," said Momma, when I got home next day, "and how was it at your meeting?" I could tell that she was interested, and I told her all I remembered of Rose Schneiderman's speech to us, and about the lady from England, and how Mrs. Blankensmith believes that women should be able to vote for themselves and show their opinions.

Not very many weeks after that Arnold and I came home from school and Momma was not there. This was the first time this had ever happened! At first I was worried for Momma. But the girl explained that Momma had gone out. A lady called up on the telephone, she said, and then Momma went out. To a meeting.

"So," said Momma, taking off her hat and sticking the hat pin into it before she put it away, "just this morning Mrs. Blankensmith called to ask would I come to a meeting for equal votes for women. And I thought to myself, if my daughter is going to meetings I should maybe go, too."

Until that night it was always Papa who had news from his customers to tell or who talked about politics. Tonight it was Momma talking and we were listening.

More and more there came such times when Momma would come from a meeting to tell us what she had learned. Mostly she went with Mrs. Blankensmith, sometimes she went by herself. Sometimes she went with Tante Ruth who, before she married our Uncle Benny, used to be an organizer for factory girls like herself.

We began to hear about things like that a lot, and

Momma was saying how important it was for women to vote and have a union and be educated. This gave Momma and Tante Ruth new things to talk about. Papa mostly agreed with Momma, but Uncle Mendel, who was not even married, often argued with her.

It was right in the middle of such an argument—call it better a discussion—that our telephone rang. Papa started to get up from his chair to go to answer it.

"Don't disturb yourself," Momma said. "Probably it is someone who wishes to talk to me."

Itzy with a Difference

On Friday nights when Momma lights the candles she looks beautiful and calm. On Saturday nights, when the whole family comes, that is when she is happy.

At these times, as on holidays, there are way too many of us to all sit at one table, so a second table is set. This is for the six children: I and Arnold and Sadie; Yonkeleh, Herschel, and little Rena-Rifka, who has to sit on a dictionary in order to reach the table. Yonkeleh, who is some years past his bar mitzvah, always makes a speech that he should not sit with the children, but no one pays attention and I think he really does not mind because we all admire him.

At the regular table are Momma and Papa, Uncle Benny, who sits next to Momma, and Tante Ruth next to him. Next to Papa sits our Uncle Mendel and, if he brings a lady, she might be in between. Uncle Benny is now a good friend with Solly Cohen, so he sometimes comes to those dinners. And finally the girl who is living with us will sit here with the others. There could be as many as eight people at the table. And under the table lies Pyro who is no longer a puppy but a grown-up dog.

On the Saturday that came in the middle of June, Uncle Mendel brought a young lady. Everyone was telling jokes, especially Uncle Mendel, and Pyro's tail was wagging under the table, and Uncle Mendel's Miss Eissler was laughing all the time.

For dinner we had chicken cooked in Momma's special way; dessert was a pudding with raisins that I especially liked. Afterwards Sadie was rubbing her eyes and Rena-Rifka, it was easy to see, was getting tired, too. So Momma and Tante Ruth together took the two of them upstairs. (Later, Tante Ruth would wake her up and Uncle Benny would carry her home, still half asleep.)

While the little girls were being put to bed—Sadie in her own bed, Rena-Rifka in mine—Uncle Benny, Uncle Mendel, and Papa went into the parlor. It was where they talked about politics and business and smoked their best cigars. Helenka, the girl, and Miss Eissler went into the kitchen to start to wash the dishes.

On this night Miss Eissler was telling a riddle and Helenka was trying to guess. The riddle was this: Mary is twenty-four years old. She is twice as old as Ann was when Mary was as old as Ann is now. How old is Ann? Helenka could hardly understand the words and so, when Miss Eissler finally told her the answer, it made little sense to her that Ann should be eighteen.

When my brother and Herschel and Yonkeleh decided to find a stickball game, or maybe start one up, I was then the only one left but I didn't really mind. I didn't even feel lonely. I went and got the book that I was reading and went out to sit on the stoop.

We'd had quite a lot of rain and I thought to myself how bright the trees were looking and that none of the leaves were turning dull and dry as they would in summer. I thought how pretty everything was and how much I loved our block. Even before the lamplighter came, lights came on in the houses, and I thought about the families inside, talking nicely together after their Saturday dinners or maybe playing cards.

Such thoughts and imaginings kept me from reading my book. When I finally opened it, it was too dark to read. So that was when I saw Itzy starting to cross the street.

"Arnold isn't here," I called. "I think he was playing stickball but now it's too dark for that."

"Maybe," said Itzy, "or maybe not. Or maybe they went for a soda." From the sound of his voice I couldn't tell if he was disappointed, but he didn't seem to mind.

"Well," I said. "Maybe. You want to wait with me?"

I was sorry as soon as I said it. Itzy was my brother Arnold's friend and what would we find to talk about with just Itzy and me? I couldn't think of anything to say and began to hope that Arnold would come soon, but Itzy started me talking, so that part was all right.

"Arnold says you're going to the mountains as soon as school is out."

"Yes," I said. "Like always." So that was when I told about Hoffmann House and the rooms we have there every year and Arnold playing the piano for the guests and the cow that frightens Sadie.

"I've never been to the country," Itzy said. "Not since coming to America. What color are the cows?"

"Brown," I said. "Reddish brown. That's where we get our milk from—" I was sounding as proud of them as if the cows were ours. "Thick cream too," I said. "When Papa comes to visit for a week he always pours a glass of cream and makes a spoon stand up in it to show how thick it is."

"Our Papa did the same," said Itzy, "when we had our farm."

"A farm!" I said, "You really had a farm?" All this time he'd been Arnold's friend and till then none of us had known about Itzy having a farm. So then it was Itzy's turn to talk and I learned a lot about Itzy I had not known before.

I began to like it with just the two of us talking! I even was not hoping any more for Arnold to come home. Also there was something I wanted to tell to Itzy. It was about the ten-cent piece of ice and how, when Miss Edgecomb said we should write about friendship, I had written about the way that he and my brother met.

"I should have asked you first," I said. "It really was your story."

"No," said Itzy, and the slow way he was talking showed that he was thinking, "with me, it was something that happened. You made it be a story."

We were both of us quiet after that, thinking about the difference.

After a while Itzy said, "Maybe, Rosey, you'll be a writer someday! A really famous writer!"

I tried to hide how pleased I was by saying something back. "And you," I said, "as smart as you are, could be a big professor."

"Why not a lawyer or maybe even a doctor?" Itzy was teasing, I knew.

"A doctor or lawyer or anything," I said, "except for president!"

Itzy said these last same words at the exact same

time. So, if we wanted our wishes to come true, we had to hook our little fingers together and do the next part. I started with, "What goes up the chimney?" Itzy said, "Smoke." Then we said the rest of it together: "May your wish and my wish never be broke." Then we let go our fingers and just looked at each other.

It was funny that this happened just then because I had been thinking to myself that the next time I got a chance to wish I would wish for what I wanted. No more wishing for the opposite as I did with Bogdana getting better, no more pretending to myself that I didn't care. Next time, I had promised myself, I was going to wish for Itzy to be my friend and not just my brother Arnold's. And that is what I had done.

Inside the house it was starting to get quiet. But Momma had still hot tea and cookies to offer, so the evening wasn't over.

"Look!" said Itzy, pointing. "The stars are coming out. The same stars here, and where I used to live, and where you'll be in the mountains."

"When I'll look at them I'll remember you," I said, and I meant it too.

"Maybe you'll write me a letter and tell me about the summer—if the cream from the cows is still so thick and the blueberries are good?"

Again we were both of us quiet. Looking up at a sky full of stars seemed the most peaceful thing in the

world, or maybe the whole world seemed at peace and we were part of it. The feelings were mixed in together, and maybe a little mixed up. I knew I had never felt like that before and that being there, with Itzy, was a part of it, too.

Then Momma came laughing out of the house. Miss Eissler and Tante Ruth came, too, and through the parlor window I heard our Uncle Mendel telling one last joke ("—and so the father said to him, 'Ikey, get out of the carriage!' ").

All at once it was everyone together, crowding the doorway and the steps, and saying "Good night," "Good night," "Good night," and, "Till we meet again!"

But Itzy on the sidewalk was only calling it out to me and I was answering back to him, and the sounds of our shouts and laughter curved and crossed in the middle of the air like fireworks in the night.

On the Friday that marked the final day of school a radiant Miss Edgecomb told her 6A class that she was soon to be married. Later she awarded three prizes. The first, for Deportment, was Mrs. Wiggs of the Cabbage Patch *by Alice Hegan Rice. Next, for Most Improvement, was a year's subscription to* St. Nicholas *magazine. Last of all, for Best Compositions, was a red, white, and blue pencil box fitted out with pencils, an eraser, pens, and a small wooden ruler.*

Before announcing the winner's name, Miss Edgecomb selected a notebook from the several on her desk and opened its marbled cover, revealing its very first page. The students watched her closely, some holding their breath. For those who had worked the hardest on their stories, this was the telling moment. Then Miss Edgecomb began.

" 'Uncle Benny's Wedding,' " she announced. "By Edwina Rose Sachs."

· 85 ·

Important Dates,
Names, and Events

1893 Papa (Irving Sachs) marries Momma (Elisabeth Kohane).

1894 Arnold is born.

1895 Rosey (Edwina Rose) is born.

1900 Arnold starts first grade.

1901 Sadie (Sarah Jane) is born.
Rosey starts first grade.

1902 The family moves to Hart Street.
Second grader Rosey meets Julia Blankensmith.

1903 Uncle Benny (Benjamin Kohane) marries Tante Ruth (Ruth Silverberg) and adopts her sons Herschel and Yonkeleh.

1904 Bogdana (Bogdana Zotowski) and Charlie, age 4, immigrate to U.S.A. and live with the family until they can go to Chicago.
Arnold meets Itzy Carnitzsky while buying ice.
Pyro is given to Uncle Mendel (Mendel Epstein).

1905 Rena-Rifka Kohane is born.
Sadie gets her own library card.

1907 Rosey wins the 6A award for Best Compositions.